D1108527

Haunted Spirits

Music by
Rebecca Sanborn

Illustrations by
Jennifer Cox

Sy James

HAUNTED SPIRITS

Printed in the United States of America

Illustrations by Jennifer Cox
Cover and Interior Design by Claire Flint Last

Luminare Press
438 Charnelton St., Suite 101
Eugene, OR 97401
www.luminarepress.com

ISBN: 978-1-64388-018-1

WWW.SYJAMESREADS.COM

To "Diego"

Haunted Spirits

Hal, the chocolate-colored mutt tried frantically to kick his legs. His four paws seemed frozen, or at least stuck in a gooey pile of muck. His friends were no help. On his left was Megan, a dark-skinned, wafer-thin girl who walked with a limp. On his right was Roscoe, a pale, husky lad with tiny ears, a lazy eye and an ever-present, mischievous grin. Hal whimpered as he pulled his legs free.

"Shhhh," whispered Megan.

Megan, Roscoe, and Hal the Dog tiptoed their way through the graveyard. It was a warm, Halloween evening featuring a glorious Hunter's Moon. The three friends were on their way to Grandma Polly's house.

Then out of the darkening blue, Roscoe stumbled over a headstone.

"Ouch," he cried. "That hurt. Stupid graves."

"Cut it out," Megan demanded. "It's disrespectful!"

"C'mon, they're only dead people," said Roscoe.

"They're more than that," replied Megan. "Grandma Polly said so."

"She only said that because she's going to die soon!" remarked Roscoe. "And I don't like the idea of missing out on Halloween candy. It's not fair!"

"Grandma Polly would not have asked us to come to see her on Halloween if it wasn't important. Now, be quiet!" ordered Megan.

The three made it through the graveyard and continued on to Grandma Polly's house. When they arrived, Grandma Polly was lying in bed, where she spent most of the time lately. Ninety-nine years old, Grandma Polly was weak and frail and dying of old age. She was also dying of a broken heart.

Everyone loved Grandma Polly even though she was nobody's grandma. She was kind, tolerant, and generous. She loved animals and children, even the wild ones, who acted "crazy as cuckoo birds" as she liked to say. Grandma Polly also loved tending her garden. Kids from all over would come and help her at harvest time, and they would usually leave with armfuls of freshly cut dahlias and vegetables. Sometimes, they left with yummy cookies Grandma Polly baked especially for them. Children also flocked to Grandma Polly's house to hear her wonderful stories about nine intelligent and bold girls who loved to learn and dance and sing.

Grandma Polly had summoned her young friends, Megan and Roscoe and Hal the Dog, to her bedside. She advised them to bring flashlights on this Halloween night. The reason was a mystery. The three stood inside the doorway of Grandma Polly's bedroom. "Thank you for coming," said Grandma Polly. "Come closer children. I can't speak very loudly these days, and what I have to tell you is very important. So listen carefully, because you have to help me. I'm too old now…I can't do what I have to do…what I should have done many years ago. You have to try and do it for me. I hope you can."

Grandma Polly proceeded to tell a sad, scary, and fantastic tale.

"Many years before, my eight sisters, Cleo, Mel, Tess, Urania, Ermine, Thalia, Eunice, and Callie, and I wandered the countryside—reciting poetry, performing plays we had written, studying history and the stars and planets. And we'd dance and sing. Not to brag, but I must say that I had the loveliest voice of all my sisters. We lived in a big house outside of town all alone. Our father, Zeke, and mother, Minnie, had passed some years before. But my sisters and I were all very happy. Then, one Halloween night, something very terrible happened."

Tears came to Grandma Polly's eyes. Megan and Roscoe felt uncomfortable, but leaned in closer to listen. Grandma Polly's room was silent, except for an occasional whimper from Hal. Her story continued…

One Halloween night, all nine sisters decided to go trick-or-treating. Their trek would take them through a dark forest, full of wild animals and, some said, full of ghosts and monsters. But the nine sisters were determined. So off they went, curiously taking an unfamiliar trail through the forest. To light the way, the nine sisters relied on a full moon and carried only a single torch between them, which Polly held at the front of the group. The path went on forever, and the torch eventually lost its flame. The wind and wolves howled.

"Now what do we do?" said Cleo. "I'm scared."

"Just follow me and shout out your name every three paces," said Polly bravely. "I'll start. One-two-three," she counted, trying to stay on the trail. And the sisters, in order, shouted "Polly, Cleo, Mel, Tess, Urania, Ermine, Thalia, Eunice, Callie!"

"Good!" Polly said. "Onward. Keep it going!"

"Polly, Cleo, Mel, Tess, Urania, Ermine, Thalia, Eunice!"

"No Callie?"

"Where's Callie?" Polly asked. "Eunice, where's Callie? You were next to her!"

"I don't know," answered Eunice. "She just disappeared!"

The sisters called Callie's name for some time. But she didn't answer.

"Maybe she got scared and ran back home," said Tess. "Let's all go back!"

"Dang it," Mel said. "Another Halloween bites the dust! Oh well, Callie is way more important than a bag of candy…teeth-rotting candy!"

The sisters started back home, continuing to call out their names. And one-by-one, they all vanished!

"Polly, Cleo, Mel, Tess, Urania, Ermine, Thalia!"

No Eunice.

"Polly, Cleo, Mel, Tess, Urania, Ermine!"

No Thalia.

"Polly, Cleo, Mel, Tess, Urania!"

No Ermine.

"Polly, Cleo, Mel, Tess!"

No Urania.

By this time all of the remaining sisters were crying.

"Polly, Cleo, Mel!"

No Tess.

Polly, Cleo!"

No Mel.

"Polly."

And finally, no Cleo.

Realizing she was the only one left, Polly began blindly running through the woods as fast as she could, branches and briars cutting her face and hands. Her legs felt heavy, like in a dream. Polly eventually emerged from the woods, but her relief lasted only a moment. In front of her stood a large, decrepit Haunted House.

Megan stared at the floor as she listened to Grandma Polly. Although Megan had never seen the Haunted House, she had heard the frightening stories. Roscoe wasn't convinced anything he heard about a haunted house was true, and that included Grandma Polly's tale now. Her story continued…

On the front porch of that Haunted House was a skeleton. It was laughing at Polly and taunting her. A giant eyeball in an upstairs window followed Polly's every move. Then the house turned into a gargantuan skull with rotted teeth and screamed.

"You're done for little Polly, just like all the rest!"

Polly yelled back, "Where are my sisters? What have you done with my sisters?"

"Oh, they're here with me. If only you could have saved them. But it's too late now. And you're next!"

Then came an eerie, horrible, other-worldly sound from the house. Then silence. Suddenly, the voices of Polly's sisters emerged from the house.

"Sister, we have passed. Set our spirits free! Sister, we have passed. Set our spirits free!"

Polly began to cry. She wanted to go towards the voices but was too afraid. Sobbing, Polly ran back through the forest. Somehow, she made it home, alone.

And alone in her big house is where Polly remained. She so missed learning and singing and dancing with her sisters. Polly had nightmares about that awful Halloween, and she was much too afraid to ever go back to the Haunted House. Every once in a while, she would hear her sisters moan, "Sister, we have passed. Set our spirits free!"

Polly felt so bad. Her heart ached. She felt completely broken.

And that's what brought Megan, Roscoe, and Hal the Dog to Grandma Polly's bedside one Halloween night many, many years later. Grandma Polly hoped the three friends could maybe free the souls of her sisters.

A large crow flying close to an open bedroom window began making a racket. Grandma Polly quickly stuck her fingers down her throat, grabbed her voice, which looked like a beautiful pearl, and threw it out the window. The crow caught Grandma Polly's voice in her beak and swallowed it!

"Follow me now, children!" cried the crow.

Grandma Polly smiled and nodded her head. Megan and Roscoe looked at the crow and then at each other in disbelief. Hal the Dog just whimpered a little and wagged his tail. Off they went. Limping, Megan led the way. Roscoe was starting to believe.

The first stop was Grandma Polly's garden. The crow landed on the shoulder of the garden scarecrow, which was there to protect the vegetables by frightening away critters and scavengers, including crows.

"I thought crows were scared of scarecrows," Roscoe asked.

"I usually am," answered the crow, "but Grandma Polly's voice has given me strength and courage. Now listen, there's a giant goose egg at the far end of the garden. Find it, crack it open and gather the contents."

The gang walked to the other end of the garden and saw the largest goose egg they had ever seen. Hal barked at the egg. Megan and Roscoe, following the crow's orders, cracked the egg open with their flashlights. Inside were three items: a bone, a comb, and a smoking pipe. The crow told them that the comb had belonged to Grandma Polly's mother, Minnie, the pipe to her father, Zeke, and the bone…

"Hmmm. I can't really be that graphic, even on a Halloween night," mumbled the crow. "Now proceed to the Haunted House with your goose-egg treasures. Grandma Polly's sisters are inside that Haunted House. Let their spirit voices guide you now. My job is done!"

By now the crow was hoarse, and it flew away, back to Polly's house.

"Guide us where?" asked Roscoe, now trembling in near darkness.

They headed for the Haunted House. Megan put the comb in her pocket, Roscoe put the pipe in his pocket, and Hal carried the bone in his mouth. They trekked through the densely-wooded forest. Strange sounds filled the air. Bizarre visions lurked on the path and hung in the treetops. But the three friends had a mission, and they were not going to let Grandma Polly down, they hoped. Halloween candy had long been forgotten. Voices faint, yet powerful, silenced the terror.

"Sister, we are here. Set our spirits free! Sister, we are here. Set our spirits free!"

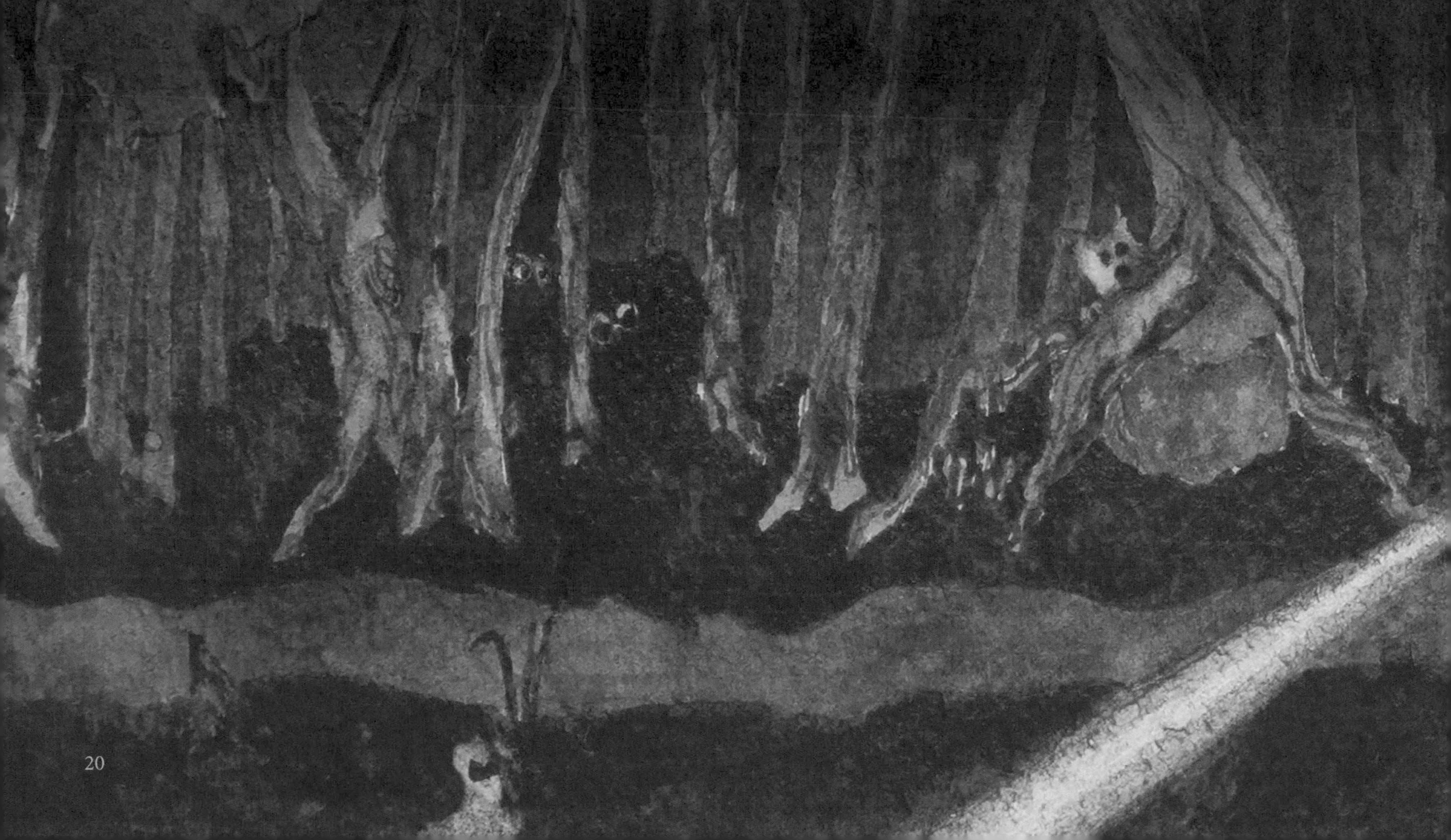

Polly's sisters were calling out! Without taking a step or moving a muscle, Megan, Roscoe, and Hal were guided and carried forward by the voices, which became louder.

"Children, we are here. Set our spirits free! Children, we are here. Set our spirits free!"

Finally, the friends came to a clearing. In front of them stood the Haunted House. The remains of several smashed pumpkins were scattered in the front yard. A strange light emanated from an upstairs window, where the giant eyeball spotted the three friends. The house then began to shake and shudder.

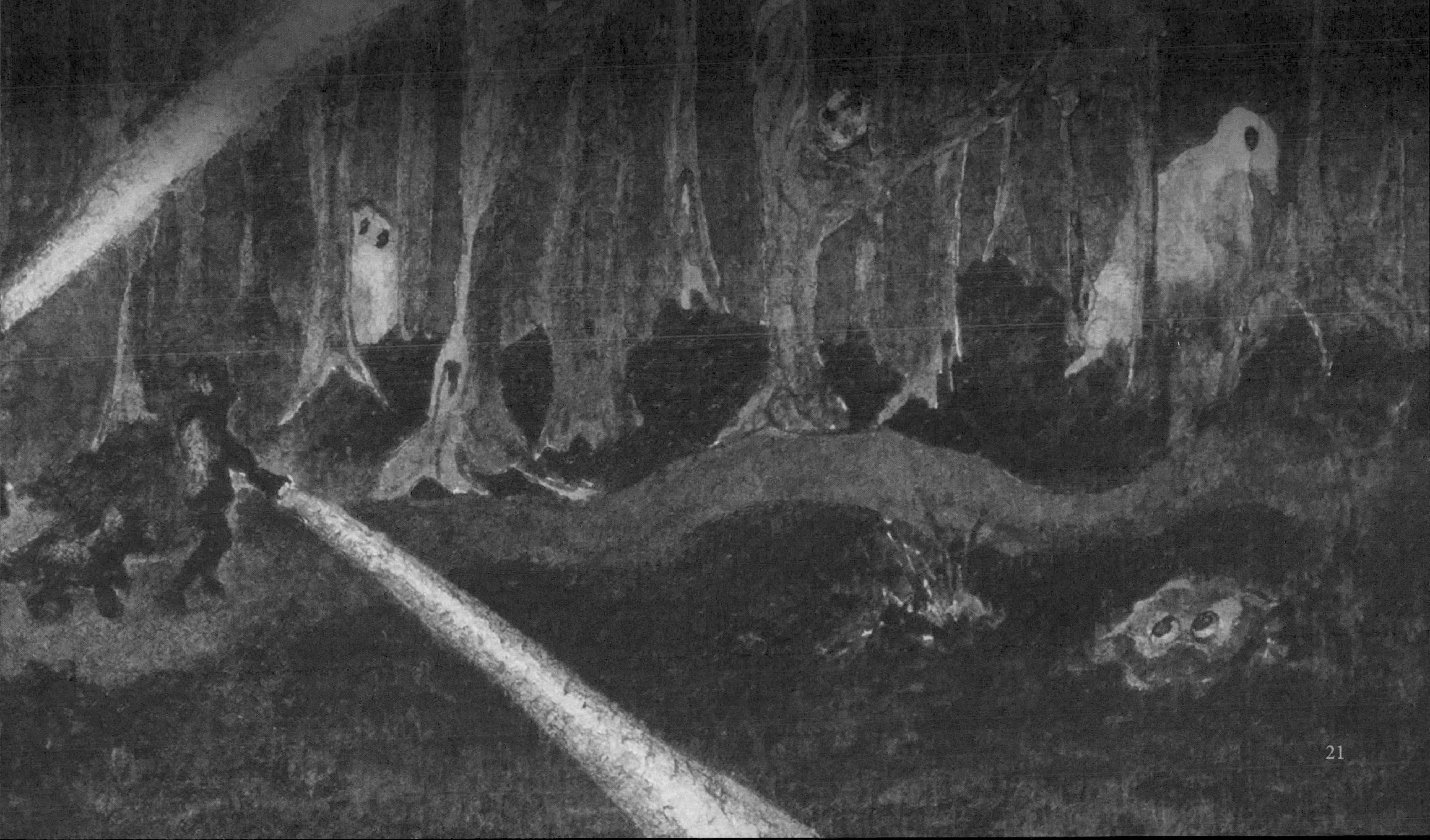

"Come inside!" demanded a skeleton dancing on the front porch. "Come here, my little tasty ones."

"I hate smart-alecks!" yelled Megan.

"Uh-Oh, ha-ha-haaaa," teased the skeleton.

Then a voice came from inside the house. "Throw the pipe at the skeleton!" It was Grandma Polly's sister Mel. "Hit that bag-a-bones with the pipe!"

Roscoe took the pipe from his pocket and heaved it farther than he had ever thrown anything. The pipe flew through the air. The skeleton caught the pipe in his mouth and, at that moment, the skeleton turned into a harmless mouse and ran away. With the giant eyeball still tracking their every move, Megan, Roscoe, and Hal the Dog ran to the house, which was no longer shaking. They climbed the porch steps and tried to open the door. It was locked.

Then another voice from within the house cried, "Use the bone to open the door!" It was the voice of sister Cleo!

Megan took the bone from Hal's mouth and inserted the bone into the lock. She slowly turned the bone. It worked! The front door opened, and the group tiptoed in. Megan, Roscoe and Hal were very frightened. But they knew they couldn't quit now. A shadowy staircase rose in front of them. Hal sniffed the air and took a few steps up the stairs.

"They must be up there," whispered Megan.

Slowly, the gang ascended the staircase. At the top of the stairs were three snarling, drooling beasts…part human, part hyena, part horrible. The beasts were standing guard in front of a purple door. Saliva dripped from the beasts' fangs. The three friends huddled together as the ghastly, gnarly beasts moved menacingly towards them.

"What do we do now?" cried Roscoe, his lazy eye, frozen in place.

"I don't know," answered Megan, who had begun to cry. "I think this is the end of us. We're sorry, Grandma Polly. We tried. We really, really tried."

Then the voice of sister Tess called out, "Use the comb. Pluck the nine teeth on the comb with your fingers."

Megan followed Tess' instructions, and the most haunting music emerged from the comb. The monsters suddenly stopped snarling and settled down, as if they were hypnotized. Then the comb jumped out of Megan's hands, and it split into three equal parts, with three teeth on each part.

"Now each of you…you too, dog," ordered Tess, "take a comb and brush the beasts."

Holding the comb firmly in his mouth, Hal the Dog approached the first beast. It was scary! And he hated getting his mouth and nose so close to the beast. It stunk worse than skunk! Hal held his breath and proceeded to comb the monstrous head of the first creature. A lullaby, sung by the imprisoned sisters, further calmed the beasts.

All the stars have gone to sleep, the quilt of clouds is soft.

And the wind she sings to them, holding them aloft.

All the children go to sleep, and their cats and dogs.

Horses snore so quietly, honey bees saw logs.

All the creatures go to sleep, and the dogs and cats.

Even turtles and the crows and the furry bats.

All are dreaming deep, all have gone to sleep.

It worked! The first beast fell asleep. Megan approached the second beast. Luckily she was able to hold the comb in her hand and not in her mouth. Megan lulled the second monster to sleep with her gentle grooming. Then Roscoe took his turn with the third. Soon all three beasts were in a deep slumber, as quiet and cuddly as newborns.

Then sister Callie said, "Now count to three, three times!"

Roscoe and Megan began to count, and Hal barked along. "One, two, three…one, two, three…one, two, three!"

1, 2, 3!

Suddenly, the purple door burst wide open. A fantastic golden light poured into the room. It was wonderful! The eight imprisoned spirits of Grandma Polly's sisters emerged from the light partly transparent, smiling with faces like angels. For a moment, the sister spirits floated above the three friends and then magically merged into one spirit. Comet-like, it flashed past Megan, Roscoe, and Hal, who jumped onto the tail of the one, sister spirit. They were all whisked out of the Haunted House and over the countryside.

Finally, the sister spirit swooped through Polly's open window, gently dropping the three friends in her room, then hovering over Polly's bed.

"We did it, Grandma Polly! We did it!" cried Megan and Roscoe, brushing themselves off. Hal barked for joy.

"Thank you my wondrous, wonderful friends," said Grandma Polly. "I thought I could count on you! Now it's time for me to join my sisters. I've missed my sisters so much. Their spirits are finally free thanks to you, and I am old and, like everyone, must die. And it is my time. I love you. I love you. Don't be too sad. I will always be with you. Just take time to listen, and you will hear my voice, our voices… forever…free!

Grandma Polly died. At that moment, the spirits of her eight sisters transformed into a cone of beautiful, multicolored rings above her body. When Grandma Polly's spirit was released, it joined her sisters forming a ninth ring and, together, the rings spun out of the window and into eternity.

Megan, Roscoe, and Hal the Dog watched in wonder. They felt great sadness and joy at the same time. And they listened to nine sisters singing clearly and powerfully with love on Halloween night.

THE END

Sy James

AUTHOR & VOICE ACTOR

Sy James is a Pacific Northwest artist, raised in the Midwest and reborn in San Francisco. Music has always helped James hear words and see pictures… Sy's child heart was broken when his friend, Isadora, moved across the bay. James spent many years overseas. After attending the premiere of "Le Sacre du Printemps," Sy returned to America and worked in the silent film industry… A voice actor for decades, James used those skills, reading to children in bookstores and daycare centers. These story times led to Sy's musical fairy tales.

Jennifer Cox

ILLUSTRATIONS

Jennifer Cox is an artist living in an impossibly magical world with a bearded man, who reminds her of a crow, a ginger-haired teenage boy, a fat, gray cat, and a mouse named Mr. Mouse. It's a charmed existence and may be a dream, but she's okay with that.

Rebecca Sanborn

AUDIOBOOK MUSIC

Rebecca Sanborn is an artist born and raised in the green cradle of Portland, Oregon. She plays in four bands. When she is not composing, she works on novels and paintings of half-withered fruit. Currently, she is being destroyed and recreated daily by her numinous infant daughter.

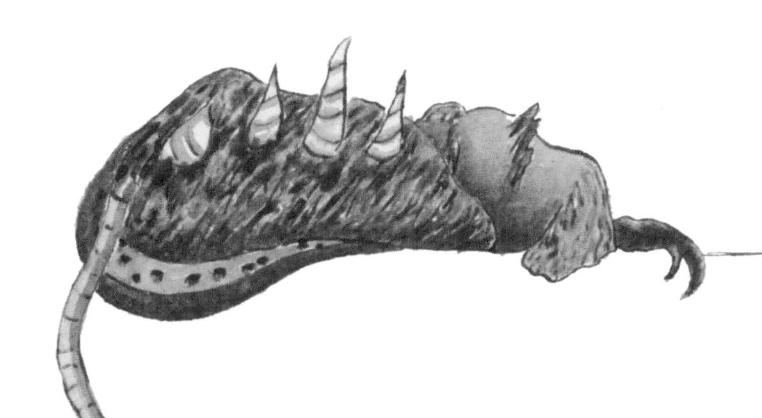

AUDIOBOOK DOWNLOAD!

www.SyJamesReads.com/download

Enter Code: HAUNTEDSPIRITS

CPSIA information can be obtained at www.ICGtesting.com
Printed in the USA
LVIW010813271018
594914LV00006BA/19